JASON
Rat-a-tat

JASON
Rat-a-tat

COLBY RODOWSKY

Pictures by Beth Peck

FARRAR STRAUS GIROUX • NEW YORK

Text copyright © 2002 by Colby Rodowsky
Illustrations copyright © 2002 by Beth Peck
All rights reserved
Distributed in Canada by Douglas & McIntyre Ltd.
Printed in the United States of America
Designed by Nancy Brennan
First edition, 2002
1 3 5 7 9 10 8 6 4 2

Library of Congress Cataloging-in-Publication Data
Rodowsky, Colby F.
    Jason rat-a-tat / Colby Rodowsky ; pictures by Beth Peck.— 1st ed.
        p.   cm.
    Summary: Jason's brother, sister, and parents all play baseball or soccer
or tennis, but until his grandfather buys him a drum, Jason doesn't want
to play anything.
    ISBN 0-374-33671-7
    [1. Drum—Fiction.   2. Individuality—Fiction.   3. Grandfathers—Fiction.
4. Family life—Fiction.]   I. Peck, Beth, ill.   II. Title.
PZ7.R6185 Jas 2002
[Fic]—dc21

                                                                99-54085

For Jane Conly

and

Doris Gwaltney

Contents

Jason   3

At the Ball Field   9

When Granddad Comes   19

The Parade   28

Unpresents   35

Bang Clatter Crash   42

Sam   50

Rat-a-tat-tat   61

JASON
Rat-a-tat

Jason

"Hurry up, Jason. I want you to get your home-work done, and then it will be time to go to your brother's game." Mrs. Miller looked around the door to Jason's room. "Okay?"

"O—kay, Mom," said Jason. He was staring down at the list of spelling words he was supposed to use in sentences—*ocean, horse, giraffe, carnival.* He picked up his pencil and tap-tap-tapped it against the edge of the metal lamp-shade, making a gentle tinny sound. He grabbed a can of bottle caps off the corner of his desk and shook-shook-shook it hard. Then he wrote his "ocean" sentence. *I swim in the ocean with whales.*

Jason played the lampshade again. Rat-a-tat-tat. He shook the caps. He wrote his "horse" sentence. *I rode my horse up into the sky.*

Jason crowded the word "blue" in front of the word "sky" in the horse sentence. He opened his desk drawer and took out a cardboard cylinder from a used-up roll of toilet paper he had found in the trash. He tootled a little song through it and wrote another sentence. *I rode a giraffe on the merry-go-round at the carnival.*

Rat-a-tat-tat. Shake shake shake. Tootle-loo. Jason made the sounds again and felt especially proud of himself for using two spelling words in one sentence.

"Jason, are you ready?" his mother called from downstairs. "It's almost time to go."

Jason played the piano along the edge of his desk. Plink plink plunk plunk—plink plunk plink. But mostly he thought about how, now that it was spring, his family was always in a hurry. The reason they were always in a hurry was that everybody in the Miller family (except Jason) loved ball games. Any kind of ball games.

His brother, Andrew, who at eleven was two years older than Jason, played baseball. His younger sister, Emily, who was six, played soccer. Jason's dad coached Andrew's baseball team and, along with the rest of the family, watched the Baltimore Orioles on television. Sometimes he even played baseball himself with other men from the neighborhood. Jason's mother coached Emily's soccer team. And she played tennis.

Even Barney the dog played ball.

It seemed to Jason that, especially in the spring, his entire family was forever going to one game or another. Andrew and Jason and Emily were always rushing to finish their homework so they could get to a game on time. They would all hurry home after the game, stopping

long enough to pick up a pizza and then gobbling it down so they could get their showers and go to bed so they could wake up early and get to school on time. After school there would be practice or another game.

It made Jason feel out of breath just to think about it. Even though he really liked carryout pizza, during baseball and soccer season he sometimes longed for his mother's spinach lasagna. He missed his father's homemade chili.

And it often seemed that all around him Jason heard the sound of a ball. Thunk, boing, ping. Big balls, little balls, hard balls, soft balls. Fuzzy yellow tennis balls and black-and-white soccer balls. When the thunk boing ping would get too loud, he'd empty out his trash can onto the floor and turn it upside down and play rat-a-tat-tat on the bottom.

"Jason, we have to leave for the game." This time, when his mother called from the foot of the steps, her voice sounded firmer than it had before and a little bit impatient.

"I'm coming," said Jason. He grabbed a ruler from the desk and went out into the hall and down the steps. All along the way he thwacked the ruler against the spindles of the banister. Thwack thwack thwack. He half closed his eyes as he went, listening to the song he was making.

At the
Ball Field

When the whole family was in the car and almost ready to go, Mrs. Miller said, "Did you bring something to do, Jason? Did you bring a book, or a pad of paper and some markers? Did you bring one of the magic tricks you got for your birthday?"

"No, but that's okay. I don't need anything," said Jason.

"But wouldn't you have more fun if you had something to do?" his mother went on. "Sometimes when I look over to check on you, you're not even watching the game. I don't want you to get bored. Well, I guess Stevie will be there, won't he?" Stevie, who was Jason's best friend, often came to the games because he had a brother who played on Andrew's team.

"Yeah," said Jason. "But I don't get bored anyway." He wanted to tell his mother how he liked to watch the clouds bunched together in the sky, and how they sometimes looked like camels. Before he could get the words out, though, Mrs. Miller was talking to Mr. Miller about whether Billy Adkins should play catcher or third base.

"And another thing," said Jason, leaning forward against his seat belt and waiting for a pause in his parents' conversation. "Remember how I told you that Stevie and I started building this really cool fort behind that giant tree next to the bleachers? We found about a ton of rocks down by the stream and these really leafy branches that are going to be the roof once we get walls." By this time they had pulled into the parking lot and his mother was hurrying every-body out of the car. She was busy gathering up water bottles and lawn chairs and sweatshirts. And she didn't hear him.

As soon as they were out of the car, Andrew ran off to join his team, the Giants, in the bull pen, and Emily found a crowd of girls playing soccer on the next field over. Jason's father stopped to talk to the umpire. Jason's mother began writing the players' positions in the team notebook.

Stevie was waiting for Jason at the edge of the parking lot and the two of them went off to check on their fort. The leafy branches they had found a few days before weren't leafy anymore, and the ton of stones didn't look like very many. "We need more stones," said Stevie, kicking at one with the toe of his sneaker.

"We need bigger stones," said Jason. "Kind of like rocks this time. To keep the alien invaders

out." They went off to the stream, gathering the largest stones they could carry and taking them to the fort. After that, they went back and forth between the stream and the fort until they had a mound of stones that was two feet tall and two feet wide.

"We'll make these the foundation," said Jason, getting down on his hands and knees to pile the stones along the outline of the fort.

"We can get more branches for the roof, but first we need to make the walls," said Stevie.

"Yeah, out of something like steel," said Jason. "That'll really keep those invaders out."

"I don't know about steel," said Stevie, standing back to look at what they had done. "But my dad's got some boards that used to be shelves at home in the garage. Maybe he'll let me bring them next time. Anyway, I'm tired of doing this now. Let's go watch the game."

Stevie ran off to stand by the fence next to the

field and Jason climbed to the next-to-the-top row on the bleachers. He sat facing away from the field and listened to the swat of the bat as it hit the ball and to the voices calling, "Run, Andrew, run!" or "Way to go, Billy!" He watched the camels in the sky overhead and played rat-a-tat-tat on the seat with two sticks he'd picked up off the ground. Rat-a-tat-tat. Rat-a-tat-tat.

"Are you okay, Jason?" his mother asked when she came to check on him partway through the game. "Sometimes I worry about you."

Jason wished his mother wouldn't worry about him. He also wished she wouldn't keep asking if he was sure he didn't want to play ball. It seemed to Jason that people were always asking him that question.

Every spring and every fall, when his brother and sister signed up for teams, Mr. and Mrs.

Miller looked at Jason and said, "Are you sure you don't want to play, too?"

And every spring and every fall, Jason said, "No."

At the start of each new season, Andrew and Emily got T-shirts with PURPLE AVALANCHES or GIANTS or METS or HURRICANES written across the back. They got schedules of all their games to hang on the refrigerator door. Sometimes Jason wished he had a special T-shirt or an important-looking schedule of things to do.

But not enough to want to play ball.

"You'd have such a good time, Jason," said his mother.

"I'll bet you'd be terrific," said his father.

"Everybody plays something," said Andrew.

"And you'd get a ton of really good snacks," said Emily.

Jason answered them all in his head.

To his mother he said, *I don't think I'd proba-*

bly have a very good time, with all those balls flying through the air. With bats swinging, and Emily and her friends kicking every which way.

To his father he said, *I don't think I'd be terrific, or even very good, or even a little bit good.*

To Andrew he said, *"Everybody" doesn't play something, on account of I don't.*

And to Emily he said, *I get lots of snacks already because the snack-parents feel sorry for the brother and sister kids who don't play ball and give us stuff anyway.*

Sometimes his parents' friends or his friends' parents asked, "What do you play, Jason?"

To all those people Jason just shook his head and said, "Nothing, I guess."

Jason remembered the one time he had let his parents talk him into playing ball. He had been seven at the time, and all his friends were signing up for coach-pitch. He could still see himself standing at the plate as Mr. Greene, the coach, sent the ball zooming toward him. And he remembered the swoosh of the bat as he would swing and miss. He could see himself in the outfield during practice, waiting for Mr. Greene to send a high fly ball in his direction. And he remembered the thud of the ball as it would hit the ground in front of him.

Not long after joining the team, Jason fell out of the tree house in Stevie's back yard and broke his arm. He was sorry that he had to stay out of the tree house until his arm was healed, and that he couldn't draw or build cabins and barracks with his Lincoln Logs or tie his shoes. But he was not even a little bit sorry that by the time his arm was out of the cast the baseball season was over.

Suddenly the yells and cheers all around him pulled Jason back to the present. He turned around and saw that out on the field the Giants were jumping up and down and giving each other high fives. Mothers and fathers and sisters and brothers were clapping and chanting, "An—drew, An—drew, An—drew."

"Andrew hit a home run and now the Giants are winning," said Emily, who had come to sit on the bleachers in the row just in front of Jason.

"An—drew," yelled Jason. "An—drew." He thumped his sister lightly on the back, playing rat-a-tat-tat, rat-a-tat-tat. Until she moved out of the way.

When Granddad Comes

On a Thursday in May, Jason's granddad drove up from Virginia for a visit. He brought a large suitcase filled with enough socks and pajamas and shirts for a weeklong stay, and a plastic bag filled with gift-wrapped books for Jason and Andrew and Emily. He even brought a jigsaw puzzle with a picture of the Grand Canyon on the front for the whole family.

As soon as the presents were opened, Grand-dad leaned back on the family-room couch, closed one eye, and looked at the three children. "Great stars, that one there has grown a foot," he said, first to Andrew, then to Jason and Emily. And all three of them stood up straight, as if they really had grown a foot. "Before I know it, every one of you'll be taller than I am," Granddad went on.

"I might be already," said Emily, tugging on her grandfather's hand until he got up. She stood on a chair and was all set to measure herself against him, back to back, when Mrs. Miller came in from outside. "I hate to rush you," she said, "but it's time for soccer practice. Come on, everybody. Got your ball, Andrew? Emily, find your socks. Jason, be sure and bring something to do. Remember, Stevie won't be there today and we'll be gone for over an hour."

When they got to the soccer field, Emily ran to join her team. Andrew went off to play ball with his friend Billy. Jason climbed halfway up the bleachers and settled back. He held a tube from a roll of paper towels up to his mouth and tooted a series of deep-down notes, as loud as he could.

For a while Granddad watched the soccer practice from the sidelines. Then he went and sat beside Jason. He leaned back on the seat behind him and listened to Jason play his deep-down notes. "Well," said Jason when he was done.

"Well," said his grandfather. He stared up at the clouds (Jason was sure they were dolphins today) and told Jason about his dog, Maude, and how he had had to promise her extra walks and biscuits for when he got back to Virginia.

On the way home from practice, they stopped and picked up a pizza. They all ate it *rush rush rush* in the kitchen before hurrying to finish up their homework and get ready for bed.

Late on Friday afternoon, Andrew had baseball practice. Mrs. Miller took Granddad and the children with her, along with three water bottles, a bag of pretzels, a dozen oranges, and a couple of lawn chairs. Mr. Miller met them all at the field after work.

While Andrew and his father headed over to join the Giants, Emily ran off to do handstands under a tree.

Granddad watched Emily doing handstands. He leaned on the fence and watched Andrew's batting practice, and when there was a break, he shook hands with all the members of the team. Then he came over to where Jason was kneeling on the ground studying a crowd of ants swarming over half a doughnut. After Jason and Granddad were finished looking at the ants, they played tic-tac-toe in the dust with pointy sticks. And when Jason took his stick and played a rat-a-tat-tatty song on the side of a metal trash can, Granddad played one right back.

"You want to see the fort Stevie and I are building?" Jason asked, leading his grandfather past the tree by the side of the bleachers.

"Stevie's not here today on account of he had to go to the dentist, but the next time he comes he's going to bring a bunch of boards for the walls. If his father'll let us have them." He straightened a row of stones with his foot. "That's the foundation there—to keep the alien invaders out."

Granddad stepped back and looked first from one side and then from the other. "That's a very fine fort," he said. "Very fine, indeed. And it's a lot like one I made when I was your age."

After the practice, the whole family hurried home, stopping long enough to pick up a pizza with pineapple on the top. Which was definitely not Jason's favorite kind of pizza.

"Now, Jason," said his mother, leaning back in her chair at the kitchen table. "Your father and I have decided that it really is time for you to sign up to play some kind of ball."

"Yes," said his father. "There's soccer and softball and even lacrosse."

"But I don't like soccer and softball, or la-

crosse either," said Jason, fiddling with a left-over piece of pineapple on his plate.

"But we want you to have something to *do*," said his mother. "We hate to see you just *sit* there during all those practices. We want you to have something you really enjoy."

"But I don't just *sit* there," said Jason, twisting the bottom of his T-shirt into a knot. "I watch the camels in the sky—only yesterday they were dolphins. And I play the tic-tac-toe game with Granddad. And when Stevie's there we work on our fort."

"Tell him, Granddad," said Jason's father. "Tell him how much fun he's missing."

"The way I see it, this is between you and the boy," Granddad said. "Except, they were mighty fine dolphins up there in the sky yesterday." He winked at Jason.

Mrs. Miller sighed and stood up to gather the plates. "Well, if you won't play softball or soccer or lacrosse, I'm going to go ahead and sign you up for tennis, then. There's a new class starting over at the recreation center, and I know, once you get into it, you'll love it."

"I *won't* love it," said Jason, slumping down in his chair. "I won't even *like* it."

"Tennis is cool," said Andrew.

"Can *I* play?" asked Emily.

"We'll talk about this some more another time," their father said. "Meanwhile, you kids had better get to bed. Remember, tomorrow's a busy day. We're going to a parade in the morning and then there's a big game in the afternoon. I don't know why they couldn't have the parade on Monday, like the rest of the country. Andrew, you can keep your light on and read for a bit, but, Jason and Emily, I want you to go right to sleep."

Jason said good night to his mother. He said good night to his father. He said good night to his grandfather and thought how he liked the way Granddad's whiskers both scratched and tickled when he kissed him.

Mrs. Miller flipped on the kitchen radio and a kind of thumpety-thumpety music poured out. Jason stood for a minute tapping out the beat on the side of the refrigerator before he trailed his brother and sister into the hall and up the steps.

The Parade

On Saturday morning, everybody in the family got up early. Mr. Miller made pancakes while Andrew and Emily and Jason straightened their rooms and Mrs. Miller fixed sandwiches to eat after the parade and before the game.

"Come on, everybody," called Jason's father. "The griddle is hot and the first pancakes are ready. And we don't want to be late for the Memorial Day parade."

"Do you like parades, Granddad?" asked Jason, reaching for the syrup.

"I *love* parades," said Granddad. Then he sang an "I Love a Parade" song, and even though Jason had never heard it before, he felt as though he'd known it for a long, long time.

"I love the floats and the drum majorettes and the big brass bands," said Granddad, getting up to put his plate in the dishwasher.

"Rat-a-tat-tat. Rat-a-tat-tat-tat," answered Jason, tapping his knife against his glass—until his mother told him to stop.

Jason and his family got a place right by the curb between a mailbox and a green bus-stop bench. Crowds swirled all around them. There were people selling balloons and cotton candy and hot dogs. There were little children in strollers and backpacks and sitting on their fathers' shoulders. There were mothers and fathers and bigger kids; grandmothers, grandfathers; aunts and uncles and cousins, too. There were policemen walking up and down the street calling, "Stand back, now. The parade is coming."

Jason heard the parade before he saw it. BOOM BOOM BOOM. He heard it up past the top of the hill and bouncing off the buildings all around him. BOOM BOOM BOOM.

And Jason felt the parade before he saw it, too. He felt the BOOM BOOM BOOM in the sidewalk underneath his feet and spilling out of the mailbox and off the bus-stop bench. He even felt it in his stomach and in his teeth.

BOOM BOOM BOOM.

The first band came over the hill. Jason saw the men and women in their black pants and red jackets and their way-tall hats with plumes. He saw the horns and flutes and trombones, the little drums and the big bass drums. BOOM BOOM BOOM. He thumped the side of the mailbox in time with the music.

Next came the marchers with flags on long skinny poles, followed by baton twirlers and men in top hats and girls riding on the backs of cars. Men in kilts came along, playing bagpipes that sent a sad sort of whining sound out over the crowd. There were floats with princesses on top, and another band, and another. BOOM BOOM BOOM. Jason beat against the side of the mailbox. He stomped his feet.

And the parade kept coming. It swept over the hill and down past the spot where Jason and his family waited, and went on beyond. Scraps of music that had already passed drifted back and mixed with music from the bands just coming into sight.

Jason watched. And listened.

After a while his mother said, "This is a very long parade. I'm afraid we're not going to be able to stay until the end."

"But we *can't* leave now," said Jason.

"We're going to have to, son," his father said. "So we can have time to eat before the ball game."

"But I don't *want* to go," said Jason.

"Would it be possible to stay for one more band?" asked Granddad, looking at his watch and then at Mr. and Mrs. Miller.

"Well, okay, one more and then we really have to hurry," said Jason's mother.

Just then, over the top of the hill, came the grandest band of all. It had the shiniest instruments and the brightest blue-and-yellow uniforms that Jason had ever seen. And right in the middle there was a man beating the biggest, boomiest drum Jason had ever heard.

BOOM BOOM BOOM.

Boom boom boom, something sang inside Jason.

"All right," said Mrs. Miller, when the band had passed. "Now we really have to leave. Come on, everybody."

"But that's it," said Jason, holding tight to the side of the mailbox. *"That's what I want to play."*

"That's nice," said his mother.

"Maybe when you're older," said his father.

"Hurry up," said Emily and Andrew, both at the same time.

"I see," said Granddad. "I certainly see."

Unpresents

On Tuesday morning, when Jason came down for breakfast, his grandfather was just getting back from an early walk. "That was a good thinking walk," he said.

"What's a thinking walk?" asked Jason.

"A walk when you think about important things," said Granddad. "There are thinking walks just as there are bird-watching walks and look-at-the-sky walks and let's-talk-to-the-neighbors walks. This was definitely a thinking walk." He smiled mysteriously and picked up the newspaper and started to read.

Jason finished his breakfast and went upstairs to get his backpack. When he came down again, Granddad was busy turning the pages of the telephone book. Then he stopped and wrote something on a piece of paper.

"Hey, Granddad," said Jason. "I didn't know you knew anybody here—except us, I mean."

"Oh, I might," said Granddad. "I just might." He smiled his mysterious smile again.

On his way to school, Jason decided to have a thinking walk, too. He thought about the spelling test he was going to have that day and about the monster movie he and Andrew and Emily had watched on the VCR the night before. But mostly he thought about the parade. It was as if he could still hear the band music inside his head, and he walked to the beat, until Andrew turned around and called, "Hurry up, Jason. We're going to be late."

When Mrs. Turner, his teacher, asked who had anything for Show and Tell, Jason stood up

in front of the class. He told about the parade—
about the floats and bands and baton twirlers,
and especially about the drums. Then he sat
down and tried to listen to the other children,
though he secretly thought that what they had
to tell wasn't nearly as interesting as the parade.

But later, during art, when Mrs. Turner
played a tape so the children could draw what
they heard, Jason thumped and rapped and
tapped on his desk in time with the music.

"That's enough, Jason," said his teacher in a
jangly voice. "That's absolutely enough."

Mom and Granddad were waiting in the
kitchen when Jason and Andrew and Emily got
home from school.

"How was everybody's day?" asked Granddad.

"Who would like a snack?" asked Mom.
"Some fruit? Or maybe juice?"

There were three packages on the counter—a

small one, a middle-size one, and a very large one. Jason knew it wasn't near Christmas or anyone's birthday and he was curious about the packages. But he was more interested in telling his mother and grandfather about the spelling test and how he stood up in Show and Tell to talk about the parade. He didn't tell them about Mrs. Turner saying "That's enough, Jason" in her jangly voice, though.

Andrew told about the ball game he and his friends had played during recess. And Emily talked about the secret club the girls in her class were going to start.

"Does anybody want to know what *I* did today?" asked Granddad, pointing to the packages on the counter.

"What did you do, Granddad?" asked Andrew.

"I went shopping for some *un*presents."

"What are *un*presents?" said Emily.

"They're presents for when it's no special

occasion," Granddad said. "And if there's no special occasion, then I figure they're not really presents—so that makes them *un*presents."

"For us? Are the *un*presents for us?" asked Jason.

"Indeed they are." Granddad got up and handed the little present to Andrew and the middle-size present to Emily. He pointed to the very big present and said, "And that one's for you, Jason."

Andrew unwrapped a new light for his bike. "Oh, wow," he said. "Thanks, Granddad."

Emily unwrapped a new basket for *her* bike. "Oh, double wow—it's what I've always wanted," she said.

Jason stood in front of the very big package. He rested his hands on top of the box and played rat-a-tat-tat.

"Go on, open it," said his mother.

"Open it, Jason," said Emily and Andrew.

Granddad handed him the scissors to cut the string.

Jason pulled up one flap on the top of the box. He pulled up the other flap. Then he closed his eyes and reached down inside, moving his fingers along something flat and round.

Bang Clatter Crash

"A drum—it's a drum," said Jason in a little voice that suddenly grew into a shout. "IT'S A DRUM."

He lifted it out and set it on the table, running his fingers over the shiny red sides and across the almost white top. *It really is a drum,* he whispered. Then he carefully turned the drum over and touched the set of wires that ran across the bottom.

"That's the bottom head, and the part right there," said Granddad, pointing to the wires, "is called the snare. This is a snare drum, but for you to play it we'll have to turn it over so the batter head is on top." Granddad turned the drum as he spoke. "And then when you strike it the snare will vibrate and cause the sound."

Jason nodded and reached out to touch the drum again.

"Hey, Jason, look—there's drumsticks, too," said Emily, digging into the box and pulling them out.

"Yeah, play something," said Andrew. "Go ahead."

"Should I?" said Jason, taking a step back.

"Come on!" shouted Emily. "Or else I'll play."

"What are you waiting for?" asked Andrew.

"Try it, Jason," said his mother.

"When you're ready," said Granddad, taking a folded-up metal stand out of the box and setting it up. He put the drum on the stand and said, "It's all yours."

"Oh," said Jason, "that's cool." He took a deep breath and let it out. "Okay. I'm ready."

He stepped up to the drum and held his arms out straight, hitting with one drumstick and then the other.

Bang bang bang clatter crash.

Bang bang bang bang.

"Well, that's nice, Jason," his mother said, rubbing her hand over her forehead. "Now, why don't you take your drum into the family room. Okay?"

Granddad helped Jason set up his drum in the family room and then went out to the driveway with Emily and Andrew to help them put the basket and the light on their bikes.

Bang bang bang bang bang bang bang. Jason hit the drum. He stopped and started up again. Bang bang bang clatter bang.

Barney crept under the table and lay down with his paws over his ears.

Bang bang bang bang bang bang, Jason

played. He played it again and again and again. Bang bang bang.

"Cut it out, Jason. I can't even *think*," shouted Andrew through the open window.

Bang bang bang bang.

"Mom, make him stop," called Emily, coming in from outside. "I want to play my *Annie* tape and I won't even be able to hear it."

Bang bang bang.

Mrs. Miller came into the room. She put her hand on Jason's shoulder and waited for him to stop before she spoke. "It might be a better idea if you played the drum in your room. Don't you think?"

Jason carried the drum upstairs. Then he went back to get the stand. He set it up next to the window and put the drum on top and stood in front of it, holding his arms out, stiff as rulers. He beat the drum. Bang bang bang bang.

A terrible, clattery, ratchety sound filled the room.

Jason stared down at the drum and wondered what was wrong. In his head he could still hear a rat-a-tat-tat-tat rat-a-tat-tat song. He heard the BOOM BOOM BOOM from the parade.

He decided to try again, only this time he stepped back even farther from the stand, and held his arms even stiffer. Bang bang bang crash. Jason's fingers were starting to ache and his ears felt stuffed with noise. BANG BANG BANG. He hit the drum as hard as he could, and then he stopped.

Jason opened the desk drawer and shoved the drumsticks inside on top of tattered bookmarks and rubber bands and broken crayons. He slammed the drawer shut and pretended not to notice the trying-not-to-cry feeling that was growing in his throat.

Just then there was a knock at the door and

Granddad came in. "I've come to tell you about another part of the present that wasn't in the box," he said. "His name is Sam."

"Sam?" said Jason. "Who's Sam?"

"Sam is Sam, and he's going to come and give you lessons to teach you how to play the drum," Granddad said.

"Lessons?" said Jason, reaching out to touch the drum and hearing the rat-a-tat-tat song louder than ever. "Really lessons?"

"Indeed lessons," said Granddad. "And I've written out a schedule of all the dates Sam will be coming. Starting Monday, because your mother says Mondays will work best for everyone."

After his grandfather had gone off to his room to read, Jason went downstairs. He put the list of lessons, in Granddad's big spiky handwriting, on the refrigerator door next to the schedules for Andrew's and Emily's games and practices. He highlighted the first lesson in yellow and drew blue and red stars around the edges of the paper. Then he turned to his mother, who was washing vegetables at the sink.

"You know, Mom, I think with Sam coming and me learning to play the drum and all, that I'm not going to have time for those tennis lessons. Okay?"

Mrs. Miller laughed. She dropped the lettuce and moved over to where Jason was standing, putting her arms around him and dripping water down his back as she gave him a hug. "You know, Jason, I think you may be right. Now come along, it's almost time for Andrew's practice."

Sam

"Can't you stay till after Sam comes the first time, Granddad?" Jason asked as his grandfather was packing to go home.

"I wish I could," Granddad said. "But I've been here for a whole week and now I have to get home and pick up Maude from the kennel. I already owe her bushels of biscuits and a whole string of extra walks. But you e-mail me afterward and tell me all about it. Why, I'll bet that the next time I come you'll be playing like Gene Krupa or Ringo Starr."

"Who are Gene Krupa and Ringo Starr?" asked Jason.

"Oh, a couple of first-rate drummers—like you're going to be someday," said Granddad.

"Yeah," said Jason, thumping out a rhythm on the side of his grandfather's suitcase. "Yeah."

On Monday, when he got home, Jason told his mother about his day and showed her the book about drums he had gotten from the school library. "They're called percussion instruments, and look—here's one just like mine," he said, opening the book and pointing. "And that's the snare part, same as Granddad told me."

"That's good, Jason," his mother said. "Did you tell Mrs. Valenti in the library that you were taking drum lessons?"

"Yeah, and she said that maybe next year I could join the school band. Do you think I can?"

"I don't see why not," Mrs. Miller said. "Now, would you like something to eat before your lesson?"

"Sure," said Jason. He took an apple from the

refrigerator and went out on the front steps to watch for Sam.

It seemed to Jason that suddenly there were many more cars than usual going down his street. There was a UPS truck and a mail truck and even a moving van. There were red cars and black cars and blue cars, but not one of them stopped at his house.

Finally, a little green car pulled up and the tallest man Jason had ever seen got out. He had inky-black hair and wore jeans and a yellow T-shirt and giant white high-tops. He carried a black case with something very large inside which, Jason guessed, had to be a drum.

"You must be Jason," the man said, coming up to the steps.

"You must be Sam," Jason said.

"And you want to learn to play the drum, right?" said Sam.

"Yeah, on account of I can hear it inside my

head—the rat-a-tat, I mean—but when I go to try it, it comes out all like crash and bang. That's when everybody tells me to be quiet and even Barney the dog goes and hides. I can't *do* it," said Jason, his voice catching just a little.

"Sure you can," said Sam. "That's what I'm here for. Besides, if the *hearing* part is there, the *doing* will come later, I promise. Now let's go inside and get started."

"Hey, Mom, this is Sam," said Jason as he led the way into the kitchen. "And that's Andrew and Emily there eating cookies, and under the table is Barney."

"Hi, guys," said Sam to Andrew and Emily and Barney.

He shook hands with Mrs. Miller.

"Is that what you do all day long, teach people to play drums?" asked Emily, looking from Sam to Jason and back to Sam again.

"Only part of the day," said Sam. "The rest of

the time I teach music at Alcott High School. I'm also the moderator of the school orchestra."

"That's a lot," said Emily.

"Well, yes," said Sam. "Except that it's mostly fun, so it doesn't feel like a lot. What do you do?"

"I play soccer and I ride my bike. When Granddad gave Jason his drum, he gave me a basket for my bike. Do you want to see it?"

"I'd love to, but first Jason and I are going to have our lesson," said Sam. "I'll see it on the way out."

"Where would you like to give your lesson?" Jason's mother asked. "Upstairs, in Jason's room maybe?"

"Well, actually, a larger room would be better," said Sam. "I like to have space—lots of space—and bigger corners for the music to creep into and bounce off of. You know how it is."

Mrs. Miller looked as if she *didn't* know how it was, but she smiled and said, "Right here in the family room, then? How about that?"

"The family room will be great," said Sam.

Andrew rolled his eyes.

Emily put her hands over her ears.

And Mrs. Miller scrunched her mouth up and gave Andrew and Emily a look that meant she thought they were being rude.

"That's settled, then," she said. "The rest of us will get out of your way, and, Jason, you run up and get your drum."

Jason set his drum up next to Sam's larger one. "What happens now?" he said.

"First let's talk a little bit," said Sam. "Did you know that drums are some of the oldest musical instruments in the world? And that the really early ones were made out of hollow logs with animal skins pulled tight across both ends?

And that these early drums were used to signal people far away?"

"The way I do with Stevie, only on the telephone?" asked Jason.

"Yes," said Sam. "But who's Stevie?"

"He's my friend, and he has a tree house and we make forts in winter and this spring we've been working on one down at Andrew's ball field that's made of stones and branches instead of snow." Jason stopped for a minute and closed his eyes. He pictured himself standing in front of his open window late at night, sending Stevie a drum message. He could almost hear the rat-a-tat-tat skimming around the corner and down the four blocks to Stevie's house. "Could I do that? Send a message to Stevie, do you think?" he said, turning to look up at Sam.

"Probably not, unless Stevie lives right next door," said Sam. "In today's world there is too much background noise—cars and airplanes and televisions. You'd better stick to the phone."

"I guess," said Jason. "When am I going to hear you play the drum? I want to hear what it's *supposed* to sound like."

Sam picked up a pair of drumsticks and held them loosely in his hands. He stood in front of his drum and all of a sudden a wonderful rat-a-tat-tat-tat spun out into the room. Rat-a-tat-tat-a-tat. His hands moved so fast Jason had trouble seeing them. Rat-a-tat-tat. Rat-a-tat-tat. He reached over and played a rat-a-tat on Jason's drum, and then, almost without pausing, he changed drumsticks, picking up a pair with sort of brushes on the ends. Swish swush swish, whispered the drum. Swish swush swish.

"Okay, your turn," said Sam.

"I *can't*," said Jason. "Not like that."

"Not like that, not yet," said Sam. "But it's time to start." He explained to Jason that if he

pushed the lever on the lower head of the drum down, the drum would sound like a tom-tom, but if the lever was up he would hear a vibrating snare sound. He showed him how to bend his elbows just enough and how to hold the drumsticks. He told him where to stand. Then Sam beat a rat-a-tat on his drum. "Now you do it," he said to Jason.

Jason held tight to the drumsticks. He stiffened his arms and his knees felt wobbly. Bang bang bang, he played.

Sam showed him again how to bend his elbows and hold the drumsticks. "Relax," he said. "This drum won't bite you. Now let's try again."

Bang bang bang, Jason played.

"Again," called Sam. "Again."

After a while Sam pulled a green spiral-bound notebook out of his case and laid it open on the table. He told Jason the sets of lines on each page were called a staff. He pointed out the small black dots on the staffs and told him that every one of them meant a note to be played.

Dots and lines and bang bang bang swirled in Jason's head.

"I think that's enough for today," said Sam, closing the book. "You'll have a lot to remember as it is. Anyway, I'll see you next week, and meanwhile, you practice what we did today. But promise me one thing, okay?"

"What's that?" asked Jason.

"To slow down and have fun," said Sam, giving Jason a high five. "And listen to the music in your head. Now let's go outside and check out that basket on your sister's bike, shall we?"

Rat-a-tat-tat

Jason had a drum lesson every Monday. Sometimes they were at his own house, with Emily and Andrew and even Barney the dog hanging around and waiting for him to get out of the family room so they could watch cartoons. His favorite times of all, though, were when his mother took him to Sam's house and he had a chance to look at the tambourines and tom-toms and bongos his teacher had collected. He often tried to play along with Sam's Beatles and Grateful Dead tapes, but most of the time he stopped to listen. He wondered if he would ever be as good as the drummers he heard on the tapes. And just before it was time to go home, he always got to play on Sam's big drum set and even clang the cymbals.

In between times he practiced in his room, except early in the morning when everyone was asleep or when his mother and father had company. He held the sticks the way Sam had shown him, keeping his arms still, except for his wrists, and beating the drum with one hand and then the other. *Left right left right left right.*

He read the notes in the music book that told him how fast or slow to play.

He went over the parts that gave him trouble. Then he went over them again.

When Jason played the drum, there were still times when he heard bang bang clatter bang. But, more and more, the rat-a-tat-tat song began to come out.

Rat-a-tat-tat-tat, Jason played. Rat-a-tat-a-tat-a-tat.

* * *

In August, Jason and his family went to the beach with Granddad and his dog, Maude. They all stayed in a house with a big screened-in porch, and in the mornings after breakfast Jason put his practice pad on the picnic table. Rat-a-tat-tat, he played. The practice pad looked like the top part of a regular drum and made a quiet, sort of muffled sound. Rat-a-tat-tat. Jason thought about his drum at home and wished there had been room in the car for him to have brought it along.

The rest of the time, Jason went to the beach. He made sand castles with Emily and Andrew and learned to dive through waves. Sometimes he and Granddad went for walks along the water's edge. They looked at the camels and dolphins and even whales in the clouds overhead. They hunted for shells and watched the seagulls.

"When are you coming to visit us, Granddad?" Jason asked one day as they were walking. "When are you coming, so I can play the drum for you?"

"I'll be there in the fall," said Granddad, bending over to pick up a gray-and-purple shell. "And I'll be ready for a concert."

When school started, Jason signed up for the school band. Because he already had a drum and was taking lessons, Ms. Duffy, the band teacher, said he could be one of the drummers. He practiced during schooltime with the saxophones and cymbals and all the other instruments. On Mondays he still took lessons with Sam. And in his spare time, Jason and Stevie and a new boy in the neighborhood named Greg built a giant fort in the woods in back of Stevie's house.

Granddad came to visit on a Friday in October. He came in his car and brought a large suitcase filled with shirts and socks and pajamas. He brought a plastic bag filled with paperback books for Emily and Andrew and Jason, and a giant jigsaw puzzle of the Statue of Liberty for the whole family. He brought a new red ball for Barney.

After Granddad had unpacked his suitcase and had a cup of coffee with Mrs. Miller at the kitchen table, Jason went upstairs to get his drum. He put it on its stand in the family room and sat on a stool in front of it. He bent his elbows just so and relaxed his wrists. He began to play.

Jason played everything he had practiced with Sam. Rat-a-tat-tat rat-a-tat-tat.

Sometimes he tried to play really fast—rat-a-tat-BANG—and then he had to try again more slowly.

Rat-a-tat-tat-tat rat-a-tat-tat-tat-a-tat, Jason played.

When he was finished, Granddad clapped as

hard as he could. He stood up and clapped some more. He called out "Bravo."

"You'll have to come back in December when Jason's school band has its big holiday concert," Mrs. Miller said. "Maybe we can all get front-row seats."

"I wouldn't miss it," Granddad said. And then he asked for an encore.

The next morning Mr. and Mrs. Miller, Grand-dad, Andrew, Emily, and Jason got ready to go to Andrew's baseball game. They gathered up fold-ing chairs and water bottles and bags of snacks. "Grab your windbreakers, everybody. It's a little cool out," called Mrs. Miller as they started for the door.

When they got to the field, Andrew and his father headed for the Giants' dugout. Emily went off to join a group of friends who were kicking a soccer ball back and forth, and Mrs.

Miller stopped to talk to the other mothers.

Jason and Granddad climbed to the top row of the bleachers, where they watched the game and talked and studied a long, skinny cloud shaped like a string bean as it drifted across the sky. After a while, Granddad started to talk to a man sitting on the other side of him. "That's my grandson Andrew playing catcher," Jason heard Granddad say. "And that's my granddaughter Emily over there with the soccer ball. And this is my other grandson, Jason."

"Hi, Jason," the man said, holding out his hand. "And what do *you* play?"

Jason pulled open his jacket and stuck out his chest. "I play the drum," he said, pointing to the words APPLEWOOD ELEMENTARY SCHOOL BAND on his shirt.

"I play the drum," he said again.